JENNY'S MOONLIGHT ADVENTURE

Written and Illustrated by

ESTHER AVERILL

A BANTAM SKYLARK BOOK®
Toronto / New York / London / Sydney

This book is for Clarisse Bates

RL 3, 007-009

JENNY'S MOONLIGHT ADVENTURE
*A Bantam Skylark Book / published by arrangement with
Harper & Row, Publishers Inc.*

PRINTING HISTORY
*Harper & Row edition published March 1949
3 printings through May 1974
Bantam Skylark edition / February 1982*

ISBN 0-553-15145-2

Published simultaneously in the United States and Canada

---

*Bantam Books are published by Bantam Books, Inc. Its trade-
mark, consisting of the words "Bantam Books" and the por-
trayal of a rooster, is Registered in U.S. Patent and Trademark
Office and in other countries. Marca Registrada. Bantam
Books, Inc., 666 Fifth Avenue, New York, New York 10103.*

PRINTED IN THE UNITED STATES OF AMERICA

10 9 8 7 6 5 4 3 2 1

On the night of Hallowe'en, the little black cat, Jenny Linsky, waited in the living room until the clock struck nine. Then she walked softly to the window.

Her master, old Captain Tinker, took Jenny's red scarf from its hook and tied it around her neck.

"I know it's Hallowe'en," said the Captain, "and it's a special night for black cats everywhere. So anything may happen."

As he opened the window, he gave her a wink.

Jenny poked her nose out into the night and sniffed delicately. She caught the musty smell of autumn leaves and heard them stir as here and there a cat prowled by.

"The members of the Cat Club are beginning to arrive," she thought to herself. "I must go."

Jenny looked at the Captain with shining yellow eyes that said, "Thank you for tying my scarf and opening the window."

4

And she jumped lightly from the low window into the garden.

Just then the twin cats, Romulus and Remus, climbed over the fence and ran to Jenny.

"Won't we have a high old time tonight," laughed Romulus in great glee.

Jenny looked at the maple tree which stood in a far-off corner of the big garden.

"I wish Mr. President would come, so we could begin."

Remus chuckled, "Mr. President is smoking his cigar."

It was an old, old joke among the members that the President of the Cat Club smoked a cigar in his parlor after supper.

No one knew if this were really true. But everyone knew that at the correct time Mr. President would walk out of his house and take the presidential place on the Club meeting ground beneath the maple tree. He always insisted on being the first to arrive at the tree.

Tonight Madame Butterfly, the beautiful Persian cat, was supposed to entertain the

Cat Club with a Hallowe'en concert on her nose flute. It was a delicate crystal flute which she plugged into her nostrils, and by breathing through it she was able to play sweet music. This evening's concert would consist of scary witch tunes.

"No one will be late tonight," said Romulus. "Everybody wants to hear those scary witch tunes."

"Everybody wants to look for witches, too," said Remus.

Jenny's eyes began to gleam, for after the concert the Club would climb the maple tree and look for witches riding down from the mountains of the moon.

By now practically all the Club members, except Butterfly, were running around bushes and jumping in the piles of leaves.

"Where's Butterfly?" asked Jenny. "Has she climbed down the vine?"

Madame Butterfly, who lived on the second floor of a house across the garden, could only reach the ground by climbing down a wistaria vine that grew by her window. Before she could get to the vine, she had to wait for the window to be opened by her mistress.

"Butterfly's mistress came home very late tonight," Remus explained to Jenny. "But the window is open now."

Suddenly there was a squeak—then a thud. Jenny and the twins dashed to the foot of Butterfly's house. In a pile of autumn leaves lay the silvery cat.

Jenny was too frightened to speak. But Romulus said, "What's the matter, Butterfly? Are you hurt?"

"I don't think so," she answered bravely.

Remus asked, "What happened?"

"I was in a hurry," said Butterfly. "My paw slipped on some of the autumn leaves on my window ledge. I fell all the way."

"Oh!" exclaimed Jenny. "Those terrible leaves are everywhere."

Butterfly tried to raise herself from the pile into which she had fallen.

"My paw! My paw!" she moaned.

And she sank down into the leaves.

At this moment Solomon, the wise cat, ran up, bringing Mr. President.

All the Club gathered around Butterfly as
Solomon examined her paw.

"The paw is sprained," he announced. "It
must be fixed by a two-legged doctor."

"Very well," said Mr. President. "Let us
call Butterfly's mistress."

The Club stepped back from the scene of
the accident and cried "Meow" in chorus.

Madame Butterfly's mistress came out of
the house, picked her up and carried her
gently away.

A moment later a light appeared in Butterfly's room, and Romulus and Remus were
sent up the wistaria vine to report on develop-
ments. Just as the twins reached the window
ledge, the window was shut.

"No visitors are allowed," they called
down to Mr. President.

Mr. President ordered them to stay and
get the best report they could.

They peered through the window pane.

After a time the twins climbed down and said, "The doctor has come. He has given Butterfly a pill and bandaged her paw. He doesn't think the paw is badly hurt. But Butterfly's nose has begun to twitch, and he can't stop the twitching. He doesn't know that she wants her nose flute. She must have lost it when she fell."

The Club searched through the pile of autumn leaves where Butterfly had fallen.

Suddenly Jenny cried, "I've found it!"

Mr. President, in a solemn voice, announced, "The nose flute has been found.

We must deliver it to Madame Butterfly as soon as we can, to comfort her. But we have several problems.

"First of all, the windows and the doors of Madame Butterfly's house are shut on the garden side. So our messenger will have to climb over the fence, run down South Street, turn into Mulligan Street and enter the front of the house through the hole in the cellar.

"Our next problem is the dogs of Mulligan Street. They will all be out tonight because it's Hallowe'en. We must choose a speedy messenger who can dash past the dogs."

Jenny shivered.

"Oh, dear!" she thought to herself. "I hope they don't choose me. I'm so afraid of dogs."

Mr. President continued his speech by saying, "Our messenger must also be big and brave so he can fight the dogs if they capture him."

Jenny breathed a sigh of relief.

"That will never be me," she decided. "I'm speedy, but I'm not big and brave."

Then Mr. President said, "Now let us choose our messenger. He must, of course, be able to carry the flute by wearing it in his nose."

SOLOMON

CONCERTINA

MR.
PRESIDENT

The big, brave cats tried on the flute. It was too small for them. They were sorry, because they would have liked to toot it.

SINBAD

MACARONI

ARABELLA
& ANTONIO

So the little, timid cats, including Jenny, tried it on. But it was too big for them.

THE
DUKE

ROMULUS

JENNY

REMUS

"This flute was made far away in Persia for a Persian nose," said Mr. President. "It does not fit our American noses. How can we deliver it? We cannot carry it in our paws and we have no pockets."

The members looked along their sides and down their hips. Mr. President had told the truth. They had no pockets.

Jenny, however, had a scarf.

"Between this scarf and my neck," she thought, "is a place just big enough to hold the flute. But I'll not tell anyone."

The seconds passed. They seemed like hours, and into Jenny's mind crept memories of times when friends had helped her when she needed help. Deep in her heart she knew that it was now her turn to help a friend in trouble. But visions of the dogs began to haunt her.

She decided, "No, I simply can't."

Jenny looked unhappily at the ground and saw patches of bright moonlight.

"Tonight is Hallowe'en," she suddenly remembered. "I mustn't be a coward when it's Hallowe'en. I mustn't, I *mustn't*."

To her own surprise, she raised her voice and said, "Mr. President, I volunteer."

"What does Jenny volunteer to do?" asked Mr. President.

"I volunteer to deliver the nose flute to Butterfly," replied Jenny. "I'll carry it in my scarf."

Little shrieks of admiration swept through the Club, for everyone knew that Jenny was afraid of dogs.

"Jenny," said Mr. President, "do you realize that you run the risk of being captured by the dogs? What will you do if they capture you?"

"I'll do the very best I can," answered Jenny. "I'll try not to let them steal the nose flute."

"They will ask you why you are running on their street," continued Mr. President. "What will your answer be?"

"I'll tell the dogs a witch was chasing me," said Jenny.

A witch!

The members were silent. Each was thinking, "It's too early in the night for witches. But Jenny is black. Black cats have special powers at Hallowe'en. Maybe her plan will work. Who knows?"

Then Mr. President said, in a voice that was almost fatherly, "Jenny, will you please step forward?"

The little black cat stepped into a patch of moonlight. Mr. President lifted his paw and tucked the flute into her scarf.

"Jenny, the Cat Club wishes you a happy landing," he said. "Try to get back in time to help us look for witches."

"Aye! Aye!" said the members softly.

And they accompanied Jenny to the fence.

"Good luck," they whispered, as she sprang to the top of the fence and dropped from sight.

The Club could hear the pitter patter of her paws as she ran through the alley leading into South Street. The Club heard Jenny turn and enter South Street. After that the patter of her paws mingled with the soft noises of the city.

The Club returned to Madame Butterfly's back yard and waited. Meanwhile, Jenny crept down South Street.

"Oh!" she prayed. "I hope those dogs don't catch me."

Only her master, Captain Tinker, knew why she was afraid of dogs. He had found her in the street when she was a tiny orphan and a dog was chasing her. The Captain had taken her to his home to live.

"That was long ago," thought Jenny. "Long ago and this is now and Butterfly must get her flute."

Jenny kept repeating, "Butterfly must get her flute."

This helped to keep up Jenny's courage. She tried not to think of the dogs of Mulligan Street. She tried not to think of Rob the Robber, who was the leader of their gang. *Butterfly must get her flute.*

As Jenny neared the corner of Mulligan Street, she could smell catnip oozing from the Toy and Catnip Shop. Although the shop was closed, the whiff of catnip cheered her. As she turned the corner, she felt almost safe, for there was not a dog in sight. Half-way down the block, which looked peaceful in the moonlight, stood the house where Madame Butterfly resided.

Suddenly a bark tore through the night. This bark was answered by another. Jenny fled toward Butterfly's house as fast as her black legs would carry her. Before she reached it, Rob the Robber blocked her path. Another dog rushed from behind. The rest of the gang, which seemed to have risen out of the street, ran on each side of her.

As the dogs surrounded Jenny, Rob the Robber growled, "Halt! We have captured a valuable prize. Let us stop right here and ask her a few questions."

Rob the Robber looked at Jenny.

"Why were you running on Mulligan Street?" he demanded.

Jenny, in a trembling voice, replied, "A witch was chasing me."

Her heart almost stopped beating during the silence that followed.

One dog grumbled, "It's too early for witches."

"Oh!" thought Jenny. "This is the end of

me. Butterfly will never get her flute un-
less . . ."

Jenny turned to the moon for help. The
moon had never looked so big and clear and
powerful. Jenny could see all the mountains
and their cliffs and shadows. Her paws
tingled with excitement.

"This is Hallowe'en. This is my night.
This is my moon," she decided. "I can make
anyone believe anything."

She gazed at the dogs with her yellow eyes
and said, "The witch has flown back to the
sky. Can't you see her riding way up there
between the mountains of the moon?"

The dogs stared at the moon.

"We can't see any witch," they muttered.

"But," said Jenny in a mysterious voice,
"maybe if you close your eyes and bark three
times at the moon . . ."

The dogs closed their eyes and barked
three times. When they opened their eyes
they still could not see a witch. And Jenny
had vanished!

She had squeezed through the hole in Madame Butterfly's house and was climbing the stairs. Fortunately the door of Butterfly's room was open, and the beautiful cat was alone, lying on a bed all covered with ribbons and lace.

"Here is your flute," whispered Jenny. "We thought you might need it."

"My precious flute," smiled Butterfly. "How I've been longing for it. I was afraid I had lost it. Now I'm sure I'll get well."

"I wish you were well enough to come with us tonight," said Jenny. "We're going to miss you. Everyone sends love."

"What wonderful friends I have," murmured Butterfly. Then she cocked her ear, looked at Jenny and asked, "Why are the dogs barking at my house?"

"They're barking at me," laughed Jenny. "They captured me and I escaped."

"Oh, Jenny!" exclaimed Butterfly. "Why did you run such a risk? Did you do it just to help a friend?"

"Yes," answered Jenny, shyly.

Madame Butterfly gave a happy flourish with her bandaged paw.

"I'd like to jump right out of bed and dance the Persian mazurka," she declared. "But it's almost time for the witches to ride, and I'm sure the Cat Club is waiting for you.

29

As my window is closed, you must go to the attic.

"Above the step ladder is a loose shingle which you can push up with your paw. Then you can crawl onto the roof and down the wistaria vine."

Jenny crept to the attic, pushed up the shingle; crawled onto the roof and looked far down into the garden.

At the foot of the vine stood the members of the Cat Club. When they saw Jenny, they began to jump with excitement. She could see Mr. President motioning them to stand still.

"That's just like Mr. President," thought Jenny. "He's afraid my friends will bother me and make me fall. But I'll not fall."

Jenny dug her claws into the trunk of the vine and began to climb down carefully.

As she passed But-
terfly's window, she
called, "Whoo hoo."

Butterfly tooted her
flute.

Jenny continued to
climb down until she
was within jumping
distance of the ground.
At this point, she let
go the vine and leaped
safely into the Club.

"Jenny!" cried the
members. "Jenny de-
livered the flute! Now
our friend, Butterfly,
will get well."

Then the Cat Club ran to the maple tree,
scrambled up into its branches and began

to look for witches riding down from the
mountains of the moon.